for Maddie, Piper and Riley – KC

Thank you to my children Ava and Max, and my nephew Eddie, for being my inspiration – LT

STRIPES PUBLISHING
An imprint of Little Tiger Press
1 The Coda Centre, 189 Munster Road,
London SW6 6AW

A paperback original
First published in Great Britain in 2016

Text copyright © Katrina Charman, 2016
Illustrations copyright © Lucy Truman, 2016

ISBN: 978-1-84715-715-7

The right of Katrina Charman and Lucy Truman to be identified as
the author and illustrator of this work respectively has been asserted by
them in accordance with the Copyright, Designs and Patents Act, 1988.

Printed and bound in the UK.

10 9 8 7 6 5 4 3 2 1

Poppy's Place

Trouble AT THE CAT CAFÉ

ILLUSTRATED BY
LUCY TRUMAN

KATRINA CHARMAN

Stripes

Chapter One

"There are more cats in this house than people!" Isla's mum grumbled as she searched for somewhere to sit that hadn't already been claimed by a cat. "Sorry, Benny," she said, lifting the tortoiseshell cat off the armchair. She placed her on the floor and flopped into the chair.

Benny gave a disgruntled meow and jumped on to the beanbag beside Isla.

Isla tried her best to look sympathetic, but

she couldn't help smile. Gran was moving in for good, they had a house full of cats, and best of all, they were going to open Poppy's Place – their very own cat café. Isla didn't think she could be any happier. She smothered a giggle as one of Benny's kittens attacked a pom-pom on Mum's slipper.

Mum wiggled her foot, trying to shoo the tiny kitten away, but caught the attention of another kitten who pounced on the other slipper.

"We need to get organized," Mum sighed. "It's time we made some real plans for Poppy's Place."

"I've already made a few notes," Isla said. "Maybe we should have a family meeting?"

Mum nodded. "Good idea."

Isla had said a *few*, but she had nearly filled her cat notebook with lists and ideas and plans for their home-made cat café. She'd been itching to get going, but with her starting secondary school, Mum's busy veterinary nurse job at Abbey Park Vets and Gran's big move, they hadn't had time to do much.

"Palmer family meeting!" Isla yelled.

"What's the big emergency?" Her older

sister Tilda wandered into the conservatory, tapping away on her phone.

Mum gestured to the ever-growing number of cats, who seemed keen to join in with the meeting. "Er, the fact that our house now contains more cats than people."

"It's time to make Poppy's Place happen!" Isla cried.

Before Tilda could respond, Milo swooped in wearing his new superhero outfit. Gran had made him a Catboy costume with a black cape and a black mask with pointed ears. A long tail peeped out from beneath his cape. Isla suspected that part of the reason Milo loved it so much was because the mask hid his hearing aid.

"Do not fear, *Catboy* is here!" Isla's little brother announced, racing over to the kittens.

Isla couldn't help laughing – since Benny's

surprise kittens had been born, Milo was almost as cat-crazy as she was.

"I've been helping Gran make jam tarts," Milo said, giggling as the four kittens licked at his fingers. "They love jam."

There was a small meow as Poppy padded into the conservatory, followed by Gran carrying a tray of freshly baked tarts and a steaming pot of tea.

"Did you show everyone Poppy's new trick?" Gran asked Milo, setting the tray down.

Milo leaped up and held out his hand. He wiggled his fingers and Poppy jumped up, tapping his hand with her nose. Milo grinned. "Poppy loves jam, too!"

"She's amazing," Isla said, leaning over to give Poppy a hug before grabbing two of the jam tarts, still warm from the oven.

One of the best things about Gran moving in was all the baking. Her cakes and biscuits were a hit with the whole family, as well as their friends and neighbours. Isla knew the yummy treats would make the perfect addition to Poppy's Place. People who didn't (or couldn't) have a cat of their own could spend time with their favourite animal *and* enjoy a cup of tea and a slice of one of Gran's delicious cakes.

"Shall we get started?" Isla asked eagerly, giggling as Roo licked at the crumbs on her jeans. She reached out and picked up the small grey cat, settling him beside Benny on the beanbag. "Why don't you sit up here?" she said, stroking his ears. "Hopefully Benny will be a calming influence on you!"

Isla grabbed her notebook and found the *Plans for Poppy's Place* page. "I've made a list," she told her family.

Tilda rolled her eyes. "You love making lists almost as much as you love cats."

Isla stuck out her tongue in reply.

"It's time we made plans to get Poppy's Place up and running," Mum said, shooting Tilda a warning look. "Otherwise it'll never happen. Besides, we need to do something about all these cats."

"It might be a good idea to give everyone a job," Isla said. "Gran … you and Milo could be in charge of the menu and anything to do with food and drink."

"Can we have brownies on the menu?" Milo asked. "They're my favourite. Oh, and lemon slices, and flapjacks, and—"

"I'm sure we can have all of those," Gran chuckled.

"Tilda … you could take charge of the website and publicity," Isla suggested.

Tilda glanced up from her phone. "I've already started actually. I've made a holding page for the website and I've added a page on my blog where people can sign up to find out more about Poppy's Place and the cats."

"That's great!" Isla said, impressed.

Tilda gave her a little smile. "Maybe you can write some cat profiles?"

"Yes! And that would fit in perfectly with *my* job … I'm going to be the Creative Director."

Milo crinkled his nose. "What does that mean?"

"It means that I'll be in charge of decorations, choosing toys for the cats, making posters… I've designed one poster already."

Isla showed them a sketch with the words *Poppy's Place* surrounded by pictures of Poppy and the other cats.

"It's a bit rough at the moment, but you get the idea. I thought it could go in the front window."

"That's wonderful," Gran said.

Isla grinned. She had spent ages trying to get the cats' noses right, so she was pleased Gran approved.

"What does that leave me with?" Mum asked.

Isla looked at her notebook. "Er … finance and forms."

Mum made a horrified-looking face.

"How about Chief Organizer?" Gran suggested, winking at Isla.

"That's perfect!" grinned Isla. "It's the most important job of all."

Mum frowned. "It's going to be a lot of work."

"We just have to be organized," said Isla confidently. "I'm sure we can open by the end of half-term."

"Half-term!" Mum spluttered, choking on her tea.

"We could have the grand opening on the second Saturday – that'll give us the whole week when we're off school to do all the finishing touches," Isla said.

"That only gives us … *five* weeks!" Mum cried. "I was thinking more like next year."

Isla gaped at Mum. "What about all the homeless cats in need of a forever home? Poppy's Place isn't just a solution for *our* cat crisis, but for all the other cats who need help."

Isla looked at Poppy, who was now curled up happily on Gran's lap. Poppy had arrived at Abbey Park Vets as a stray after she'd been hit by a car. Gran and Isla had convinced Mum to let Poppy come home. And that had been just the beginning. Slowly Poppy had worked her magic on Mum and they'd ended up taking in Roo, Benny and Benny's four kittens.

"I hate the idea of cats like Poppy having nowhere to go," Isla said sadly.

"I do, too, Isla," Mum said. "But at least there's the cat sanctuary – Dolly does an amazing job."

"But it's always full," Isla argued. "What about our idea of helping cats find their forever homes through Poppy's Place? We could see if the sanctuary has any cats that might be suitable to come here?"

"We do have rather a lot of cats already," Mum pointed out. "But I guess we could plan a visit to Dolly's." She glanced at Milo and the kittens and whispered, "The kittens *will* be old enough to leave Benny in a few weeks' time."

Isla's heart sank. She knew the day would come when the kittens would have to leave, but they'd all fallen in love with them, especially Milo, and she'd hoped Mum might let them stay for Poppy's Place. She glanced at Gran who was watching Milo with a sad look on her face. Isla knew she felt the same way.

"Is the meeting finished?" Tilda asked. "I'm meeting Gabriella in town in half an hour."

"Not quite," Mum said. "I need a list of my own."

She went to the kitchen and returned with a whiteboard they used for messages and reminders. She wiped it clean then scribbled *Poppy's Place – Where? When? How?* at the top.

"I think the conservatory is the best room for the café," Mum said. "Agreed?"

Everyone nodded. The conservatory was Isla's favourite room. It ran along the entire back of the house, overlooking the garden. Isla imagined it transformed – with comfy sofas and beanbags for the customers, and toys for the cats to play with. There was already a cat flap which led out to the garden so the cats could come and go as they pleased.

"Mr Evans has volunteered to help us with the garden," Gran said. "So on sunny days we can have tables out there, too."

"Great," said Mum, scribbling notes on the whiteboard.

Isla frowned as a thought occurred to her. "When are we actually going to be open?" she asked. "We're at school during the week and you're at work, Mum. That only really leaves weekends."

"Gran's here all the time," Milo said.

"I can't run Poppy's Place on my own, Milo," said Gran, ruffling his hair. "Besides, where would I be without my kitchen helper?"

"I think weekends are probably all we can cope with," Mum said, adding a note to the whiteboard. "At least to begin with."

Isla nodded, wishing she didn't have to go to school. She'd much rather stay at home to help out with the cats and Poppy's Place.

"I read online that other cat cafés have rules about how many customers they can have at one time and how long they stay for, so we should definitely write some rules for Poppy's Place," Tilda said. She held up her phone and showed them an image of a cat-shaped teapot. "And we could sell cat-themed stuff like this as well, and maybe cushions and cat calendars."

Mum frantically scribbled down Tilda's ideas.

"That's all part of my job as Creative Director!" Isla interrupted.

Tilda ignored her. "Then there's all the equipment we're going to need – coffee machine, tablecloths, cups, saucers…"

"That reminds me, I've got a few bits of furniture coming from my old house first thing tomorrow," Gran said. "Maybe some of it would be suitable for Poppy's Place? I've got some garden furniture, too."

Mum stared at the whiteboard covered in notes.

"This is going to take a lot more planning than I thought … not to mention money. We need to start with the important things, like filling out forms and applying for a licence – without that we might not even be allowed to open."

"We can take care of everything else, though," Isla said, bubbling with excitement. She couldn't wait to start – it was going to be so much fun! "So can we open at half-term?" she asked. "Please."

Mum didn't look convinced.

"Honestly," Isla said. "You do the forms and leave the rest to us. Poppy's Place will be up and running in no time."

Chapter Two

When Isla came downstairs for breakfast the next morning, she found the hallway piled high with furniture.

"Furniture fort!" Milo yelled, pushing past Isla to dive beneath a table.

"Oh, sorry, Isla," Gran said, peering over the top of an upside-down armchair. "I didn't realize the furniture was being delivered quite so early! The kitchen's a bit blocked off at the moment. You'll have to get breakfast at school."

Isla groaned. It wasn't that she didn't like Langford High – even though she'd only been there a week, starting secondary school hadn't been as scary as she'd thought it would be … so far she'd only got lost once. But making new friends was a lot harder than she remembered. Her best friend Grace was at the same school but she was in a different class and it wasn't like primary school at all.

"I thought you said there were only a *few* bits being delivered?" Mum puffed, trying to drag a large chest of drawers into the lounge.

Gran frowned. "There seems to be a lot more than I remembered."

"Never mind," Mum said. "I'm sure we'll find space somewhere."

"Talking of space," Tilda said, appearing at the top of the stairs, "maybe it's time Isla found somewhere else to sleep…"

Since Gran had come to stay, she'd been sleeping in Isla's room, while Isla shared with Tilda. It wasn't an ideal solution, but Isla had enjoyed spending more time with Tilda – even if her big sister was on her phone for hours on end.

"I thought you liked having me in your room," she said, feeling a little hurt.

Tilda gave Isla an apologetic look. "It's just so cramped."

"You'll have to make do, I'm afraid," Mum said. "We don't have any spare space."

"But there *is* another room in the house," Tilda insisted.

Mum slapped a hand to her head. "You're right. I can't believe we didn't think of it sooner!"

"Where?" Isla asked, confused.

"The attic!" Mum and Tilda said together.

"I'm *not* moving into the attic!" Isla shuddered, imagining the cold, dark attic, full of cobwebs and pigeon poo.

"It's a lovely room," Mum said. "We've only used it for storage because we didn't need the extra space – until now."

Isla scowled. "Why can't Tilda move up there?"

"I have a room already," Tilda said. "Besides, your things are still packed up so it makes sense."

"A lick of paint and a clear-out, and it'll be nice and cosy," Mum promised. She leaned over the chest of drawers to kiss Isla on the head. "Now, off to school."

"Don't forget the forms!" Isla reminded her, ducking beneath a table to the front door.

The morning crawled by and Isla was relieved when the lunchtime bell finally sounded. She hurried out of the classroom and headed for the courtyard, desperate to see Grace and tell her all about her disastrous day.

As if double PE hadn't been bad enough, she'd forgotten her kit. Isla had hoped she would be allowed to sit the class out, but Mr Bennett the PE teacher had made Isla search through lost property to find some suitable clothes. She'd ended up wearing a mouldy-smelling green T-shirt, and a pair of tiny white shorts. She had felt so embarrassed.

As Isla waited for Grace, she jotted down more notes for Poppy's Place. She'd found a cat café online that also rehomed cats. On their website, they had a list of rules similar to those Tilda had mentioned, so Isla was adapting them for Poppy's Place.

Our Cat Rules

1. Don't pick up the cats — let them come to you

This wouldn't be a problem for Benny — she loved nothing better than a lap to curl up on. The tricky part was going to be when the customer tried to leave!

2. No children under the age of 5

They couldn't risk any of the cats being grabbed at or chased, which led Isla to rule number three...

3. No tail pulling

Lucy, the vet at Abbey Park, said it was vitally important that the cats were happy.

Isla looked up and sighed. If Grace was any longer, there wouldn't be any tables left. She noticed a girl from her form called Bonnie sitting with two other girls. One was tall with short blond hair, the other had the longest bright red curls she had ever seen. Isla took a

deep breath and closed her notebook. If she
wanted to make friends, she was going to have
to actually start trying.

"Hi," Isla said shyly, approaching their table.

The tall girl whispered something Isla
couldn't quite hear, making the red-headed
girl laugh. Isla hesitated and looked at Bonnie.
"I ... I think we're in the same form – 7B?
You're Bonnie, right?"

Bonnie nodded. "I—"

"What *is* that?" the tall girl interrupted,
pointing at Isla's hand.

Isla looked down. The top of her pen had a small furry cat on a spring. It bounced wildly back and forth as she frantically stuffed it into her backpack.

"Nothing," Isla squeaked, wishing that Grace would turn up.

"A cat! How cute," the tall girl taunted.

The red-headed girl laughed and looked at Bonnie, who gave a weak smile. Isla's face flushed as she fumbled with the zip on her backpack. In her panic to get away, she pulled a little too hard and the entire contents spilled on to the ground.

Horrified, Isla scooped up her things as quickly as she could, blinking hard to hold back the tears. She hurried away, sure that everyone was staring at her, and found a quiet corner on the other side of the courtyard. She leaned against the cold wall and took out her lunch. She'd been starving earlier, but now Isla felt sick.

Where was Grace when she needed her?

"How was school?" Gran asked as Isla curled up on the sofa with Poppy.

"Fine," Isla mumbled, searching her backpack for her notebook.

Her heart sank as she realized she must have lost it when she dropped her things in the courtyard. All her notes and plans for Poppy's Place … gone. It had been the worst day ever.

Gran gave a little frown, then her face brightened. "Your mum's got a surprise for you."

"Where is she?" Isla asked.

"In the attic."

Isla groaned and plodded upstairs as slowly as she could. She couldn't stop imagining creaky floorboards, dusty old boxes and spiders in every corner.

"She's home!" Milo yelled, scuttling excitedly down the attic stairs to give Isla two thumbs up. "I wish I could sleep up there, but Mum says I'd make too much noise on the wooden floorboards!"

"Come on up!" Mum called in a muffled voice.

Isla anxiously climbed the narrow stairs.

Mum was standing in the middle of the room wearing tatty denim overalls and a scarf tied around her head.

"What do you think?" she asked. "I still need to find a home for those boxes and put up some blinds, but you can paint the walls whatever colour you like."

Isla looked around the room, her eyes wide. The attic was huge – twice the size of her old room. There wasn't a cobweb or speck of dust in sight, and Mum had wound some old Christmas lights around the wooden beam which crossed the ceiling. It looked magical.

"I put your bed beneath the skylight," Mum said, "so you can see the stars at night."

"It's amazing!" Isla breathed.

There was a thump on the stairs behind them and Tilda appeared. "What are you—"

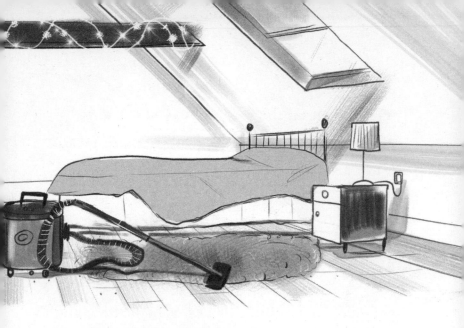

She gave a little squeal. "You never told me the attic was this big!"

Mum smiled sweetly. "You never asked, Tilda."

"But – it's *way* bigger than my room!"

"I know," said Mum. "It was such a nice idea of yours to let Isla have all this space."

Tilda's mouth opened and shut a few times. Isla covered her own mouth, trying not to laugh.

"About that," Tilda started. "I know Isla

wasn't keen on the idea, so maybe I could move up here instead? I mean, it would be a bit of a sacrifice, but if it made Isla happy…"

Mum gave Isla a hug as she, too, tried not to laugh. "That would be *very* generous of you, Tilda, but it's up to Isla to decide. Isla?"

Isla glanced around. "It is amazing up here," she said, "but I think I'd rather be downstairs with the cats. They might not be able to climb those stairs. Thanks, Tilda."

Tilda smiled. "What are sisters for?"

"That's settled then," said Mum. "We can do the big switch at the weekend, and you can both paint your rooms if you like."

There was a sudden yell from Milo downstairs. Mum rolled her eyes. "I'll be back in a minute."

Isla's phone buzzed in her pocket with a text from Grace:

Sorry couldn't meet at lunch. Had drama club. Totally forgot! G x

Isla paused. *She forgot?* Isla would never forget to meet Grace if they'd made plans.

No problem, Isla replied. *Fancy coming over on Saturday with Ayesha for a room decorating party? x*

Count me in, Grace replied. *And watch this space for some amazing news! x*

Isla shoved her phone in her pocket, wondering what Grace had to tell her. Hopefully it wasn't that she'd joined more clubs and Isla would have to eat alone every lunchtime for the rest of her life.

"What's up?" Tilda asked, plonking herself down on the bed.

"Nothing," Isla mumbled.

"You can have the attic if you want…"

Isla shook her head and sat down.

Tilda gave her a quizzical look. "So what's the problem? You don't seem your normal annoyingly bouncy self."

Isla shrugged and buried her feet in the shaggy rug Mum had placed beside the bed.

"Going to a new school and making new friends is harder than I thought it would be," Isla admitted.

"It was the same for me when I started at Langford High."

"Really?"

Tilda nodded. "Did something happen at school?"

Isla shook her head quickly. She didn't want Tilda feeling sorry for her.

"Well," Tilda said. "Just be yourself. You'll soon make friends. And I'm here whenever you need a chat."

Isla gave Tilda a small smile. "You know," she said, changing the subject, "another downside of being up here is that you can't smell Gran's baking – I'm sure she mentioned something about chocolate cupcakes."

"Better get down there before Milo eats them all," Tilda laughed, and raced for the stairs.

Isla followed. There was nothing that Gran's baking couldn't fix.

Chapter Three

"I have the *best* news!" Grace squealed, hugging Isla as soon as she opened the front door.

It was Saturday morning. Mum had gone on a health and safety course in preparation for opening Poppy's Place, and Gran, Milo and Tilda were out shopping for supplies. Isla was a bit disappointed not to be with them, but Grace and Ayesha were coming over to help her decorate her new bedroom. She couldn't wait to make it hers, and finally be able to put up all her old cat posters.

"What is it?" laughed Isla.

Without stopping to answer, Grace rushed into the conservatory and scooped up one of the kittens. "Dad said I can adopt Lady Mewington!" she said, stroking the tiny kitten. "I've been going on about it for weeks, and last night he finally said yes!"

"That's brilliant!" Isla exclaimed. "We can have cat playdates. I can't believe your dad changed his mind!"

Grace's dad was allergic to cats – or at least that's what he told Grace. Isla suspected he just wasn't that fond of animals, but she knew how persuasive Grace could be when she set her mind to something.

"It's a Christmas miracle," Grace sang, covering Lady Mewington's head in kisses.

Isla laughed. "It's September!"

"Close enough." Grace grinned.

"Will you change her name?" Isla asked.

Milo had been allowed to name the kittens and had chosen Lady Mewington for the little girl, and Captain Snuggles, Fluffboy and Dynamo – his favourite – for the boys.

"Lady Mewington seems to fit her quite well," Grace said. "She's such a little princess."

Isla looked at the tiny kitten who had captured Grace's heart, and had to agree.

There was another knock at the door. Grace reluctantly put Lady Mewington down and the girls hurried to the front door. Ayesha was standing on the doopstep struggling with a large box of wallpaper, paint pots and brushes.

"We can use whatever we want," Ayesha said, as Isla and Grace helped her in with the box. "I wasn't sure what colour you'd want so I brought them all."

"Your mum won't mind?" asked Isla.

Ayesha's mum was an artist. She painted
whole walls or massive sheets of white fabric,
creating colourful murals. When they were
younger, she'd helped the girls make their
own art by dancing across the garage floor,
their bare feet covered in paint. The footprints
were peeling and faded now (and Isla couldn't
believe that their feet had ever been so small)
but it was one of Isla's favourite memories.

Ayesha shook her head as they set the box

down in the conservatory. "She loves it when I show an interest in painting – even if it is just decorating. You could use some for Poppy's Place, too."

"Thanks!" said Isla, opening the door to the garden and leading her friends outside. She couldn't wait to fill them in on all the plans. "Come and see what I've been working on. This will be the grand entrance." Isla gestured to a small, painted wooden sign nailed to the side gate which said, *This way to Poppy's Place.*

Grace squinted. "Shouldn't it be bigger?"

"A bit more eye-catching?" Ayesha agreed.

"It's a work in progress," Isla said defensively. "I'm going to make a bigger sign when I get the chance. Actually, Ayesha, do you think your mum would help me with a present for my mum's birthday?"

"Sure," Ayesha said.

"Thanks," Isla said. "I want to do something special and I've just had a really cool idea." They wandered back into the conservatory. "We'd better get started on the painting," Isla said. "Mum left us some old T-shirts so we don't get messy, and I've got plastic sheets to cover the furniture."

They carried everything upstairs and surveyed Isla's new room. Mum and Tilda had already moved Tilda's things into the attic and the bedroom looked so much bigger now that they could see the floor.

"Where shall we start?" asked Ayesha, levering open the paint pots and placing the lids on newspaper on the floor.

"Why don't we try a few different colours?" suggested Grace.

Isla chose deep pink, while Grace went for a light blue and Ayesha picked green.

They each painted a small patch of wall then stepped back to admire their handiwork.

Grace wrinkled her nose. "Not green. I don't think it's your colour, Isla."

Isla nodded in agreement.

"The pink looks nice," said Ayesha.

"It does," Isla agreed. "But maybe not for the entire room."

"Oh no!" Grace cried, pointing behind Isla.

Isla turned to see a path of tiny pink paw prints splattered across the cream carpet, at the end of which was Roo, looking very pleased with himself.

"Roo!" Isla scooped him up before he could do any more damage.

"How did you get up here? Just look at the carpet! How are we going to clean this off?"

"Wash it?" Grace suggested.

"Water might make it worse," warned Ayesha.

The three girls stared at the carpet. Isla needed to think of something – and fast. Mum was going to kill her if she caught sight of the paw prints. Especially as the cats weren't allowed upstairs.

Isla gasped. "I've got an idea!"

She handed Roo over to Grace and raced up the wooden stairs to the attic, reappearing a few moments later with a rolled up rug.

"Please let it fit!" Isla whispered, hoping that Tilda hadn't become too attached to the shaggy rug.

Isla let out a sigh of relief. It was just big enough to cover the paw prints.

"Perfect," Grace said, passing Roo back to Isla. "I'm sure no one will notice."

"Now, we'd better clean up this bundle of trouble before he does any more damage," Isla said, carrying Roo to the bathroom.

Cats, Isla quickly learned, do not like water.

"Stay still!" she squealed, trying to hold on to a very wriggly Roo, while Grace and Ayesha gently rubbed at his paws with warm water.

"It could have been worse," Grace said.

Isla looked down at the dripping wet and very unhappy Roo, then at her own clothes, which were just as soaked. "How?"

"It could have been black paint!"

Isla laughed and kissed Roo's head. "Poor thing. He looks even smaller when his fluffy fur's all wet."

She dried Roo off with a towel and took him downstairs, making doubly sure that all the cats were accounted for before shutting the kitchen door.

"Right, let's get started," she told her friends, reappearing in the doorway. She glanced at the walls. "Let's go with one pink wall, one yellow wall and one blue wall."

As they began rolling the paint on to the walls, the conversation quickly turned to school.

"My new school is huge," Ayesha said. "There's an indoor swimming pool *and* a state of the art computer suite. And everyone seems really friendly. What's Langford High like?"

"I'm still getting used to it," Isla said, pausing to push her glasses back up her nose. She wondered whether she should tell them about the incident with the mean girls in the courtyard, but decided not to. She just wanted to forget all about it.

"I wish you were in more of my classes, Grace. You've made loads of new friends already," said Isla.

Grace stopped painting to gave Isla a hug. "I'm sure you'll make new friends, too. It's only been a couple of weeks. Why don't you join the drama club?"

"Drama's not really my thing," Isla said. "Now if there was a cat club…"

The girls laughed.

"Oh!" Ayesha gasped. "I almost forgot. Guess what I pass on my bus route every day?"

"A sushi restaurant?" Isla guessed. Ayesha loved sushi.

Ayesha shook her head. "A cat café!"

"Really?" Isla said.

"I couldn't believe it! I *was* a bit worried

at first," Ayesha admitted, "about there being another cat café so close. But it's way over the other side of the city."

"I can't believe I didn't know about this!" Isla cried. "I think we should visit," she decided. "For research purposes." Her mind was racing. If Mum visited an actual cat café, maybe she wouldn't be so worried about everything they still had to do (and it might encourage her to get on with the forms).

"Good idea," said Ayesha.

"They'll never get you to leave!" Grace teased.

The girls chatted and painted all afternoon. It reminded Isla of when they were together in primary school – everything had been so much simpler.

"There," Ayesha said, putting down her paintbrush. "My wall's finished."

"Mine too," said Grace.

"It's so colourful!" Isla said, looking around.

Grace's wall was blue. Ayesha's was a sunshine yellow, and Isla's was pink. On the fourth wall, they had each painted a mini mural. Grace had painted a dancer. Ayesha, a beautiful white lily, and Isla (of course) had painted a cat.

"I love it, thank you!"

Isla pulled her friends into a group hug.

"It'll look even better when you put up your cat posters," Ayesha said.

Isla glanced at a box filled to the brim with all the cat things she had collected over the years – posters, ornaments, a paw-print blanket for her bed – then remembered the girls at school laughing at her because they thought cats were babyish.

What if Grace and Ayesha secretly think that, too? Isla worried. She pushed the box into a corner, out of sight.

Chapter four

"Tilda!" Isla whispered as she crept into the attic the next morning, trying not to wake up the rest of the house.

Mum was always reminding them that Sunday was her only day for a lie in. Although it wouldn't be for much longer, Isla thought, not once Poppy's Place opened.

"Whasgoinon?" Tilda mumbled beneath her duvet.

"You told me to wake you up early," Isla

hissed. "To work on the website – remember?"

Tilda groped at her bedside table until she found her phone. She pulled it beneath the duvet and let out a loud groan.

"It's seven a.m.! Come back in a couple of hours."

Isla would have liked a bit more sleep herself. She hadn't slept very well. It had been too quiet without Tilda snoring next to her, and even with the freshly painted walls and new rug, her room felt empty. But there was too much to do to laze around this morning, and besides, she needed to make a start on the cat profiles.

Isla yanked the duvet off the bed and Tilda gave a loud shriek.

"There's so much to do!" Isla said. "*And I was thinking we need to make plans for Mum's birthday. I've already had an idea.*"

"Fine!" Tilda snapped. "But I need breakfast first. I can't work on an empty stomach. What's your idea for Mum's birthday?"

"I thought maybe Ayesha's mum could paint her a mural for Poppy's Place – on the fence next to the side gate."

"Sounds good," Tilda said, yawning. "We should have a chat with Milo and Gran, too, to see if they have any ideas. We need to make Mum's birthday really special this year – it's the Sunday before our grand opening, and I have a feeling she's going to be working really hard to get Poppy's Place up and running. It'd be good to give her a relaxing treat."

"You're right," said Isla, her head brimming with new ideas. She left Tilda to get dressed and went downstairs. While she waited for the bread to toast, she opened Tilda's laptop to make a start on the cat profiles.

Tilda had added a holding page to the Poppy's Place website for potential visitors to register their interest and subscribe to a newsletter. Isla gasped as she saw how many people had already signed up. It was exciting and terrifying all at the same time. If that many people wanted to visit, they'd be run off their feet for months!

Isla handed Tilda a plate of toast as she came into the kitchen, then opened a new document on the laptop for the cat profiles. There was going to be a page featuring each of the cats, with cute pictures and a bit about how they'd ended up at Poppy's Place.

"You two are up early," Mum said, shuffling into the kitchen.

"So are you," said Isla.

Mum shivered and held up a pile of paperwork.

"I still haven't finished these forms – they're giving me nightmares."

"You can probably fill them in online," Tilda said. "It might be easier?"

"I've already started them," Mum said, stifling a yawn. "But first, I'm going to need a big cup of tea."

"I know what will wake us up!" Tilda grinned, fetching a large box from the hallway and dumping it on the table. "Ta-da!" she sang.

Mum glanced at the box. "A coffee machine?"

"Not just any coffee machine," Tilda said, opening the box to lift it out. "A top of the range, state of the art, all singing-all dancing hot-beverage dispenser."

Isla burst into giggles at how excited Tilda seemed over a coffee machine – that must be how *she* sounded when she talked about cats.

"It makes frothy milk and everything," Tilda said, ignoring Isla. "Who wants a cappuccino?"

"Never mind frothy milk, when did you get this? And how much did it cost?" Mum asked.

"It was my treat," Gran said, coming into

the kitchen with Poppy. "We bought it yesterday while we were out shopping. I'm more than happy to use some of my savings to get Poppy's Place up and running. Now how about that cappuccino – I'd love to try one."

Tilda flipped through the instruction booklet, then tossed it aside.

"Can't be too difficult," she muttered, plugging the machine in.

She placed a cup underneath the nozzle and pressed a button. Nothing happened.

"Don't you need to add—" Isla started.

"I know what I'm doing, Isla!" Tilda huffed, jabbing at a few more buttons.

There was a high-pitched beep and the front of the coffee machine lit up with flashing red lights.

"Is it broken?" Isla asked, her eyes wide.

"Make it stop!" Milo yelled, covering his

ears as he came to see what was going on.

"Tilda!" Gran cried, hurrying over to put her hands over Milo's ears. His hearing aid was sensitive to high-pitched sounds.

Mum quickly unplugged the machine and handed the instructions back to Tilda. "I think you need to read these," she said.

Tilda was about to argue when Gran cut in.

"Tea it is then," she said, giving Milo a hug before reaching for the kettle.

"What else did you buy yesterday?" Isla asked, jealous that they'd been shopping for Poppy's Place without her.

"Wait till you see!" Tilda ran upstairs and returned with an armful of bags and boxes.

There were placemats, cutlery sets and a bag of cat-shaped tea cosies. One of the boxes was filled with cat-covered notebooks and pens.

"To take people's orders," Tilda told them. "I thought maybe we could buy some more and sell them in the café as well."

"Ooh, brilliant!" Isla grinned, helping herself to a pen and notebook.

"Hang on," cried Mum, grabbing the whiteboard and frantically making notes. "I need to keep track of what we've bought. Anything else? Any other bits of news?"

"Yes!" cried Isla, remembering what Ayesha had told her. "A cat café has just opened on the other side of the city – we should visit."

"To steal their ideas?" Tilda said, with a wicked grin. "I like it!"

"Tilda!" Mum gasped.

"I'm joking!" Tilda said. "But it would be good to check out our competition."

"That's what I meant!" Isla huffed. "For research, obviously."

"I'll look them up and give them a ring later," Gran said, steering Milo towards the table. "Now we need to have breakfast before we head off for the swimming pool."

"Did you call the cat sanctuary about visiting?" Isla asked Mum.

Mum shook her head. "I'll ask Dolly tomorrow – she's bringing a cat in for a check-up. I'm sure it'll be fine to pop over one day after school."

Isla, Tilda and Mum sat in silence for most of the morning, each absorbed in their own task. Mum muttered to herself every now and then as she filled out the forms. Tilda took photographs of the cats and uploaded them to the website, and Isla worked on the profiles.

Meet the cats at
Poppy's Place

Poppy

Poppy is a very special cat.
With her shiny black fur and little white socks
and chest, she is not only beautiful, but smart,
too. She can give cat high-fives, jump up to touch
your hand, and is learning lots more new tricks.

Benny

Benny loves nothing better than being cuddled.
Although she was abandoned by her owner,
she has settled into her new home quickly and loves
keeping an eye on her four playful kittens ~ Dynamo,
Captain Snuggles, Fluffboy and Lady Mewington.

Roo

Roo is a fluffy grey cat. He's about eight months old, but is not much bigger than the kittens. He makes up for his small size, however, by causing maximum mischief.

Isla finished the profiles and glanced out of the window. "I'm going to make a list of things we need to do to the garden," she said, picking up her notebook.

Tilda grunted, and Mum continued to glare at the forms as if she were willing them to fill themselves out.

Isla headed outside and stood staring at the overgrown garden. It was such a mess. She knew nothing about gardening. Neither did Mum for that matter. But hopefully with Mr Evans' help, it could soon be sorted – his garden was immaculate.

"Hiya," said Sam, popping his head over the fence.

Sam, their next-door neighbour, was eleven – the same age as Isla. They'd been in the same class at primary school, but now Sam went to a posh all-boys school.

"Hi," Isla said shyly.

She hadn't seen Sam for a couple of weeks and he seemed a lot older suddenly.

"Is your cat café open yet? I need some more of your gran's cake!"

Isla grinned. "You can come over any time for that. We're supposed to be opening at half-term, but there's still so much to do," she admitted. "Just look at the garden!"

"I could help," Sam offered. "My friends, too."

"Thanks," Isla said. "We might just take you up on that."

Sam and his friends had helped Isla set up

a mock cat café during the summer holidays. It had been a huge success and had convinced Mum to open their own home-made cat café.

There was a little meow beside Isla and she looked down to see Poppy waving her paw. "Someone wants to say hello!" Isla giggled, picking Poppy up to high-five Sam. "Watch this. She's got some new tricks."

She put Poppy down and tapped her gently on the nose. Poppy followed Isla's finger, rising so that she was standing on her back legs.

"Cool," Sam said.

"Milo's a bit disappointed that she can't skateboard though!" Isla laughed.

As if on cue, Milo ran into the garden, his hair still wet from swimming.

"Mum won't listen to me!" he wailed. "It's so unfair."

Isla glanced at Sam. "Sorry, I'd better go."

"Oh," Sam said, looking a bit crestfallen. "I'll see you later, maybe?"

Isla gave him a little smile and hurried over to Milo.

"Your mum told Milo about the kittens," Gran said, joining them outside. "She's going to put up a notice at Abbey Park."

"I want them to stay with us!" Milo sniffed.

Isla's heart sank. Milo loved the kittens. It did seem really unfair – after all, Gran had Poppy, she had Roo, and Mum would never part with Benny.

"What can we do, Gran?" Isla asked.

Gran shook her head sadly. "I think your mum's already made up her mind."

Isla kneeled down in front of Milo. "I know it's sad, but it is easier to find a kitten a new home," she explained. "Lady Mewington is going to live with Grace, so I'm sure we'll see

her all the time. Remember what Mum said –
about the older homeless cats? Maybe we can
give some of them a home?"

"I suppose so." Milo sniffed again, giving
Poppy a hug. "But I still don't think it's fair."

Isla couldn't help but agree. Maybe she
could convince Mum to at least let them keep
Dynamo?

Chapter Five

"We need another family meeting," Isla told Gran and Tilda on Monday morning. "Mum *still* hasn't finished the forms – they're on the kitchen table – and we've got to organize sorting the garden and the conservatory. We're going to run out of time."

Isla also wanted to talk with Mum about the kittens. If she was going to try and change Mum's mind, she needed to do it soon, before it was too late.

"Maybe that could be part of Mum's birthday surprise?" Tilda suggested. "We could tidy up the garden so it's one less thing for her to worry about."

"What surprise?" Milo asked, wandering into the kitchen in search of food.

"Shh!" Isla said. "We're planning Mum's birthday present."

"I'm seeing Mr Evans this morning," said Gran. "I could ask him if he's free to help. I'm guessing you want to do it on Mum's actual birthday, which gives us … three weeks to get everything organized."

Isla smiled. It was so good to have Gran living with them, and brilliant to see her so much happier than she'd been a few months earlier, after Grandad had died.

"We could get Ayesha's mum round to do the mural at the same time," Isla said. She filled Gran and Milo in on her idea. "And Sam said he and his friends would help, too," she added, feeling her face go a little pink.

"The garden and mural can't be her only presents though," said Tilda. "We need to think of something special … something she'd enjoy doing that will get her out of the house. And I think I've thought of the per—"

"What's all the whispering?" Mum asked, coming into the kitchen.

"Family meeting," Isla said quickly. "Have you finished those forms yet?"

Mum gave Isla a guilty look. "I just haven't had the time," she admitted.

"Half-term is only four weeks away!" Isla said, worry bubbling up inside her.

"I'll finish them tonight," Mum promised.

"I phoned the cat café and they're going to squeeze us in on Saturday," Gran told them.

"It's called Cats, Cuddles and Cupcakes."

"Brilliant!" Isla said, hugging Gran. "I can't wait to see it!"

"Neither can I." Gran smiled. "I told the owner about Poppy's Place, because I thought she might be worried about another cat café opening up, but she was very nice about it."

Isla glanced at the clock. "We're going to be late for school!"

Tilda squealed and ran out of the front door.

Isla raced after her, but suddenly remembered her PE kit. She rushed back upstairs to fetch it, calling to Tilda to go on without her. As she set off for school, half-walking, half-jogging, Isla thought she heard a small squeak behind her.

She looked around, but the street was empty. As she continued on, she heard the squeak again and something moved inside her

backpack. Gingerly, she took off the backpack
and put it on the ground. Her heart pounded
as she pulled the zip very slowly to reveal…

"Roo!" Isla cried as he leaped out at her.
"How did you get in there?"

The school gates were a little further ahead,
and Isla heard the bell ring in the distance.

"What am I going to do with you?" Isla whispered, hugging Roo close.

She pulled out her phone and called home, but there was no answer. Gran must have already gone to see Mr Evans while Mum took Milo to school.

"You'll never find your way home by yourself," Isla told Roo.

There was only one thing for it. Hugging Roo tightly inside her jumper so that he couldn't escape, Isla ran back down the road. By the time she reached home, she was gasping for breath.

She unlocked the front door and plopped him inside. "Stay!" she told Roo, giving him a quick kiss.

She checked her watch: 8.30 a.m. Registration was about to start and it would take her ten minutes to get back to school.

"I'm going to be in *so* much trouble!" Isla groaned.

She locked the door and ran back to school.

When she reached her form room, she hurried to her desk, relieved to see that there was no sign of her teacher, Mrs Davis. Isla pulled out her water bottle with shaky hands and took a few deep gulps. As she closed the lid, she looked up to see Bonnie sitting down in the empty chair next to her.

"Mrs Davis is late," Bonnie said.

"Thank goodness!" Isla breathed. "I didn't think I'd make it."

"I keep trying to talk to you," Bonnie continued, her cheeks pink, "but you always seem to be in a big rush to get somewhere."

Isla felt her own cheeks go red. She had been avoiding Bonnie ever since the episode in the courtyard.

"I've been really busy," Isla said, which wasn't exactly a lie.

"I wanted to say sorry for the other day. Those girls were really mean to you, and you probably think I'm horrible, too, and…" Bonnie's words came out in a big rush.

Isla was a bit surprised for a moment, then she smiled. "It's OK," she said. "I understand."

Bonnie reached into her backpack and pulled out Isla's missing notebook. "You left this behind. I had a little peek inside … I wasn't snooping, I just wanted to make sure it was yours."

"Oh, thank you!" Isla said, hugging the notebook to her chest. "I thought I'd lost it. I've been racking my brains to remember everything I'd written down."

"I love cats, too," Bonnie whispered, as Mrs Davis finally appeared.

"I have seven!" Isla whispered back. "Maybe you can come and meet them?"

"Seven! Wow! I'd like that."

"One of them tried to come to school with me this morning," Isla laughed. She started to tell Bonnie all about Roo and the other cats, until Mrs Davis told them to be quiet.

Isla smiled to herself. She couldn't believe she'd avoided Bonnie just because she'd been embarrassed about loving cats. There was no reason why she couldn't love cats *and* make new friends.

Saturday finally arrived after what had felt like the longest week of Isla's life. She was so excited about their visit to Cats, Cuddles and Cupcakes, that she could hardly eat.

"Now remember," Mum told Tilda as they hurried off the bus, "don't interrogate the owners as soon as we arrive. It was very kind of them to fit us in."

Tilda rolled her eyes. "I hope they won't mind meeting the competition."

"Of course they won't. Anyway, we're not really competition," said Isla. "Poppy's Place isn't just a café – we'll be focusing on rehoming the cats, too."

"I guess so," said Mum doubtfully.

"It'll be fine." Gran saw the worried look on Mum's face and quickly ushered her towards the café.

The window had been painted with colourful cats and paw prints that led down to the pavement then continued to the café door.

"Wow!" breathed Isla as she entered the café. "Look at the cat-shaped handles on the teacups!"

"Look at all the cat toys," Milo said, his eyes wide.

"Ooh, they've got Wi-Fi," Tilda said, getting out her phone.

"Tilda!" Mum hissed. "Will you please put it away! Just this once!"

A striped tabby cat padded over and Isla kneeled to give him a stroke.

"That's Tigger," said a lady, appearing

behind them. "You must be the Palmers – table for five?"

Mum shook the woman's hand. "I'm Sarah Palmer, this is my mum Maria and my children Tilda, Isla and Milo."

Isla grinned. "This place is amazing!"

"I'm glad you like it." The lady smiled. "I'm Julia. My husband Bob is in the kitchen. We've only been open for a few months, but as you can see, we're very popular already."

Isla looked around, taking in every detail. Almost every table was taken with happy customers chatting away and drinking tea and coffee. And there were cats everywhere! Some of them lounged on small sofas and in baskets, while others played on platforms with feathers dangling from them. The best part, though, was that they all looked so happy – the customers *and* the cats.

"It's even better than I imagined!" Isla said.

"Isn't it?" said an old lady sitting at a table nearby. "We're not allowed pets where I live, so this is wonderful. I do love cats, don't you?"

Isla nodded, and followed Mum and Julia to a table covered with a cat-print tablecloth.

"What made you want to open a cat café?" Mum asked.

"It's a funny story, actually," said Julia. "I used to leave food outside for a stray cat who often wandered into my garden. He was a bit wary of strangers and would never come to me when I called, but the poor thing was so skinny I had to do something. One day, I noticed him eating the food I'd left, so I went outside and sat with him. The next day, I left the food as usual and later that day he came back, and this time he let me stroke him. A couple of days later he returned with a cat friend, so I left a bit of extra food for them both, then a week later, they returned with five kittens in tow!"

"Just like us!" Milo gasped.

"I've always wanted to work with cats, but wasn't sure how, until Tigger and his family showed up."

Tigger padded over as if on cue, rubbing himself against Isla's leg.

Julia laughed. "You'd never believe he was once such a skinny little thing. Now, who'd like some tea and cake?"

The morning flew by in a wonderful blur of cats, cake and laughter, then more cake and cat cuddles. Milo spent the entire time playing with the cats. Isla scribbled down as much as she could, making notes on the cat toys and drawing sketches of the café, while Mum and Gran chatted with Julia and Bob, and Tilda took some photos on her phone.

On the way home, Isla felt more excited than ever about Poppy's Place.

"Wasn't it wonderful?" she said to Mum.

"It really was," Mum said. "I think we might actually be able to do this – make a success of Poppy's Place."

"That's what I've been telling you all along!" Isla grinned as she felt the excitement of the day bubbling up all over again. "And our visit has given me even more ideas," she said. "Especially in terms of the cat toys and play areas – we really need to think about those…"

Mum laughed and gave Isla a hug. "We're supposed to be ticking things off the list, not adding to it! But you're right – the cats' welfare is our priority so we need to make sure Poppy's Place works for them. We can go to the pet shop to look at toys and baskets tomorrow if you like? It'd be a start…"

Isla whooped in reply.

"At least the forms are done. I'm so relieved about that!" Mum said. "And I've arranged for us to visit Dolly's after school on Tuesday."

"It's all falling into place," Isla sighed happily. "Everything looks set for half-term and the grand opening of Poppy's Place."

Chapter Six

"I've got some bad news," Mum said, when Isla and Tilda got home from school on Tuesday. "I've had a letter from the council asking me to fill in a new form – another one! And they may do an inspection, too."

Isla gaped at Mum. "Does that mean we can't open Poppy's Place?"

"Let's hope it doesn't come to that. But we're going to need to make sure that we're ready in case they do send an inspector."

Mum gestured to her laptop. "So much for my day off," she grumbled. "I'm doing the new form online – hopefully it'll be a lot quicker."

Isla peered over Mum's shoulder and frowned. There were at least five different web pages open.

"I'll give you a hand," Tilda offered. "I'm sure I can crack it while you're at Dolly's."

"Thank you! Have a look at what I've done so far," Mum said. She glanced at the clock. "We should go, Isla. Dolly's expecting us in twenty minutes."

Mum waved Milo in from the garden and hustled him and Isla out of the front door. "If we hurry we can catch the four o'clock bus," she said.

They dashed along the pavement, with Isla and Milo moving ahead in a little race.

Suddenly Milo sprinted off, leaving Isla

trailing behind.

"Don't run off, Milo!" Mum shouted.

"I don't think he's wearing his hearing aid!" Isla cried, her heart thumping as Milo ignored their shouts to stop and headed straight for the busy main road.

"Milo!" Mum yelled, chasing after him. "Milo! Stop!" she gasped, grabbing Milo's hand as she finally caught up with him. She made sure he could see her face as she spoke. "Why aren't you wearing your hearing aid?"

"I took it off when I got home from school, because it was itchy," Milo sniffed, his lip wobbling. "Sorry."

He could still hear without it, but found it difficult when there was a lot of noise or people talking at once.

"You're going to have to hold my hand," Mum said. "It's too busy."

Milo pouted. "I'm not a baby!"

"Tell you what," Isla said, "I'll hold Mum's other hand."

Mum smiled and gave Isla's hand a squeeze.

"Just this once, though," Isla whispered.

"Dolly's Farm!" Isla said, reading the sign outside the cat sanctuary. "Do they have other animals, too?"

"A few, I think," Mum said, "but it's mostly set up for cats."

Isla had never been to a cat sanctuary before, so she wasn't sure what to expect. She'd imagined something like Abbey Park Vets, with a reception area and holding cages, but Dolly's Farm was nothing like that.

Milo raced over to the paddock, his earlier

tantrum forgotten.

"They have llamas!" Isla said.

"Actually, they're alpacas," someone said behind her, with a chuckle.

Isla turned to see a very tall woman wearing blue overalls and muddy wellington boots.

"Hi, Dolly," said Mum, her face breaking into a smile. "Dolly runs the cat sanctuary," she explained to Isla and Milo.

"Along with a few kind volunteers," said Dolly. "You must be Isla. I've heard you're a bit of an animal lover yourself."

Isla nodded. "Especially cats!"

"And this must be Milo. Would you like to stroke one?" Dolly asked, nodding towards the alpacas. "They're very friendly."

"Can we?" Milo asked, wide-eyed.

"If that's OK with your mum?"

Mum nodded.

Dolly opened the gate and they followed her to a white-haired alpaca. Its fur felt how Isla imagined a sheep's coat felt. Soft, but a bit rough. Definitely not as nice as stroking a cat.

"So," said Dolly, "tell me all about your big idea."

While Dolly took them on a tour of the farm, Isla, Milo and Mum told her about Poppy's Place and their plan to rehome rescue cats.

Dolly nodded enthusiastically. "Cats are our most regular guests," she told them.

"Guests?" asked Isla.

Dolly gave her a sad smile. "I call the animals guests because we only look after them until they find their forever homes. Some of them have been guests here for a lot longer than others."

She led them into a small office with a

desk, sofa and a couple of cat beds. In one of the beds was a sleeping ginger cat.

"Like Oliver here," Dolly said. "He's been with us for almost two years since his elderly owner passed away. We think he's about twelve years old. Nobody wants to adopt a cat that old, so he'll probably be with us for the rest of his days."

"Ah!" Isla cried, kneeling down to stroke him. "I can't believe nobody wants him."

Oliver slowly opened one eye to look at Isla, then went back to sleep, purring quietly.

"And this is Blossom," Dolly said, introducing Milo to the tabby cat on the sofa. "She's been here a while, too. We do our best, but as you can see, we're full to bursting. It's getting more and more difficult to find space for the animals, so your idea of a cat café sounds wonderful."

"We're looking for cats who are very
sociable," Mum explained. "Maybe two years
old or more, as I know it's easier for you to
find homes for kittens."

"We already have four kittens," Milo grumbled, "but Mum wants to get rid of them."

Mum crouched in front of him. "Look at these cats who don't have homes, Milo. Wouldn't it be great if we could find them a home at Poppy's Place? Everyone wants a kitten because they're small and cute, but older cats like Oliver might not ever find a home. We don't have room for the kittens *and* some new cats."

Milo glanced at Isla and she gave him a little smile. It was now or never.

"It does seem a bit unfair, though," she started. "Gran has Poppy, I have Roo, and you have Benny…"

"Benny belongs to all of us, Isla," Mum said. "She's just more attached to me."

"And you're attached to her," Isla argued.

"Just like Milo is to Dynamo. The first thing you do when you get home from work is look for Benny."

"I suppose you're right," Mum said.

Milo nodded, giving Isla a hopeful look.

"OK, OK." Mum sighed. "If you promise you'll try to keep your hearing aid on … *and* you promise to take very good care of him – no crazy hug-a-cat schemes or teaching him to ride a skateboard…"

Milo ran at Mum, giving her a huge hug.

"…Then you can keep Dynamo."

Milo let out a loud whoop, startling Oliver, who hobbled off to find somewhere quieter to take his nap.

"Now that's settled, shall we see the other cats?" Dolly asked, laughing.

"Yes, please!" Isla said, beaming as Milo ran over to hug her, too.

Dolly led them through a series of rooms. She hadn't been joking when she said they were full to bursting. Isla didn't think she'd ever seen so many cats in one place before.

Each room had a cat flap leading outside, and each cat had their own bed with blankets and toys. Isla was glad they weren't kept in cages. She wasn't sure she could bear to see all those beautiful cats locked up.

"We're far enough out of the city that there's not much chance of them going near main roads or getting into trouble, and they can roam wherever they like," Dolly explained. "I do get quite a few mice and birds as little gifts, though."

"Our cat Roo gave me a mouse once," Milo said proudly.

"It was still alive," Mum whispered to Dolly.

They spent some time getting to know the cats and finding out which of them might have the best chance of being rehomed at Poppy's Place. After half an hour, Mum and Dolly had drawn up a shortlist.

"I'd like to come back with Abbey Park's vet, Lucy, to get her opinion," Mum told Dolly. "If we get our licence, perhaps we could take a new cat every month, depending on how the adoption scheme goes?"

"Perfect," Dolly said. "Then I'll have space to take in new cats."

"Great," said Mum. She turned to Isla and Milo. "Time to go, you two. We need to get home for tea or we'll be in trouble with Gran!"

"Can I say goodbye to Oliver before we go?" Isla asked.

The thought of Oliver not having a real home made Isla want to cry. She found him on a warm spot on the kitchen floor and gave him one last hug.

"I wish I could take you with us," Isla whispered into his fur.

Oliver purred softly in reply. She kissed his head, then said goodbye.

"Mum," Isla said slowly as they headed to the bus stop.

Mum sighed. "I recognize that voice."

"I can't bear to see Oliver left behind. Dolly's brilliant and she looks after the cats so well, but it's not the same as having a real home. He'd be no trouble and I bet he'd love all the hugs and cuddles in the cat café."

Isla waited for Mum to argue that they had no space or couldn't take on such an old cat, but she simply said, "OK."

Isla blinked. "We can adopt Oliver? Really?"

Mum laughed. "I don't know what's wrong with me lately, but yes, we can adopt him. If Dolly agrees."

Isla grabbed Milo and they jumped up and down laughing. She couldn't quite believe it.

Not only were they keeping Dynamo, but they were getting another cat as well!

Mum grinned, then held a finger to her lips as she took out her mobile to answer a call.

Isla took Milo's hand as she watched Mum's face turn white.

After what seemed like forever, Mum rang off. "There's an emergency at work," she told them. "We need to get to Abbey Park as quickly as we can."

Chapter Seven

The bus journey to Abbey Park Vets felt like
the longest half hour of Isla's life. All Mum
knew was that some cats had been rescued
from an empty house and it appeared that
the owner had gone away and left them. Isla
didn't know how people could be so mean.

"I'm going to see if I can get through to
your gran," Mum said, taking out her mobile.
"Maybe she can meet us there and take you
two home."

"I want to help," Isla insisted.

"I'm not sure, Isla. Lucy said the cats were very distressed. Sometimes people can be incredibly cruel to animals and I don't want you to get upset."

Isla took a deep breath. "If I'm going to work with animals, then I'll have to get used to it. Besides, I can keep them company – it's what I'm best at."

Mum gave Isla a small smile as she tapped "home" on her mobile. "You do have a way with cats."

Once, when Isla had been helping Mum at work, one of their clients, Mrs Morgan, had come in with her cat Bruiser after he'd got his head stuck in an empty tin. Isla had sat with Bruiser on her lap, stroking and chatting to him until he calmed down and stayed still long enough for Lucy to free him. And when

Poppy had been brought in after she'd been run over, Isla had spent ages talking to her and brushing her and making friends.

Isla knew the abandoned cats must be in a bad way, but she was determined to be strong for Mum and Lucy, and help if she could.

Gran was already waiting at the bus stop when they reached Abbey Park.

"I thought we could make bread rolls," Gran told Milo, taking his hand.

"By ourselves?" Milo asked.

"They might make a nice addition to the Poppy's Place menu," Gran said.

Milo went off with Gran, excitedly telling her about the alpacas and the news about Dynamo and Oliver.

Mum watched them leave then looked at Isla. "Ready?"

"Ready," Isla said.

They found Lucy in one of the treatment rooms. Isla gasped when she saw the tiny cat crouched and shivering on the table. She'd never seen such a skinny cat. Its fur was filthy and matted, and it made little high-pitched mewing noises as though in pain.

"What happened?" Mum asked.

"There are four cats," Lucy explained. "All from the same property. It looks like the owner left some time ago and locked the cats inside. They're malnourished, and they're going to need round-the-clock care for the next few days while I assess them properly."

Lucy glanced at Isla. "Do you want to keep the others company while your mum and I take a look at this one?"

"OK," Isla said quietly, unable to take her eyes off the shivering cat. She wanted to cry. She'd never seen an animal look so scared before.

"I've already given them a little bit of cat milk," Lucy said. "But they're so thin they can't have too much in one go, it might make them sick."

Isla nodded. "Can I stroke them?"

"I think that'll be OK. Just be very gentle and quiet. They might try to scratch or bite as they've not been around people for a while, so be careful. The poor things were terrified when they were brought in." Lucy handed Isla a pile of blankets. "Take these – we need to keep them warm."

Isla took the blankets and went to the holding cages at the back of the building. Lucy had put the cats together in one of the larger cages and Isla found them huddled against each other like one giant cat. They were just as skinny as the cat in the treatment room.

Isla opened the cage slowly and carefully placed the blankets inside, making sure to avoid any sudden movements. One of them – a tortoiseshell, like Benny – immediately crawled beneath a blanket as if it was trying to hide.

Isla pulled up a chair and sat down, lightly placing her fingers on one of the blankets. The cat closest to her was facing away from the cage door, but Isla couldn't resist reaching out to it, almost touching its tail. After a few moments, the cat glanced round at Isla. Slowly it got to its feet, turned around and settled back down, resting its head on Isla's fingers.

"Hello," Isla whispered. "You'll be OK now, I promise. Lucy and Mum will take very good care of you all."

The cat lifted its head as though it was listening, then ever so quietly started to purr. Isla moved her hand gently and stroked the cat's head. The two of them sat like that for almost an hour until Mum appeared.

"I'm going to be here for a while yet," Mum told Isla, bringing the cat from the treatment room and placing it carefully in the cage with the others. "You should probably go home and have some dinner."

"I want to stay and help," Isla said.

"You've done a great job, but it's getting late." She gave Isla a hug. "I'm proud of you, Isla. You'll make an excellent vet one day."

Isla beamed. Ever since she was little she'd dreamed of working with animals. "Do you really think so?"

"I know so," said Mum.

Mum called Tilda to come and meet Isla outside the vets – she didn't like her walking home by herself at night, even though they only lived five minutes away.

"I don't know how people can be so cruel," Isla said, as they passed the parade of shops.

"It's awful!" Tilda agreed. "Poor things."

Isla knew that sometimes people couldn't look after their pets for one reason or another, but why would they abandon them with no food or water when there were great people like Dolly around? Isla felt even more determined to make sure that Poppy's Place was a success. If they could help even a few cats, it would be worth the hard work.

"What about Dolly's Farm?" Tilda asked. "Were there any cats there who looked like they could fit in at Poppy's Place?"

Isla told Tilda all about Mum's plan for the cats including Oliver, and her amazing change of heart over Dynamo.

"Cool," said Tilda. "And Gran and me finished the extra form this afternoon. It took hours."

"Great," said Isla, feeling relieved that Mum wouldn't have to finish it later.

"*And* I've had the most brilliant idea for Mum's birthday," Tilda went on. "We can send her to a spa for the day! That way she'll be forced to relax *and* she'll be out of the way while we do our garden makeover surprise. Gran says Mr Evans is all set to help out."

"That's good," said Isla, "as I've got an idea for a fantastic cat playground which I'm hoping he can help us build in the garden."

Tilda rolled her eyes. "I might have guessed! And what about your friends?"

"They're all set," said Isla. She grinned. Mum was going to have the best birthday ever!

After dinner, Tilda showed Isla some flyers she'd designed for the grand opening. Even though Mum had warned her that they

couldn't open without a licence, Tilda had
posted the date on the website with a form
where people could request tickets.

Poppy's Place Cat Café
GRAND OPENING
VISIT OUR WEBSITE TO REQUEST TICKETS!

"There are twenty requests already," Isla
said as she read through the comments.
Everyone seemed very excited about visiting a
cat café.

"Most of the guests will be family and friends," Tilda said. "But I thought we should keep a few spare tickets for potential customers."

"Hey, there's an email from Sally Smithers! *The* Sally Smithers! From the newspaper," Isla said excitedly. "It says she's been following our blog since she interviewed us about Poppy and Abbey Park Vets, and wants to cover our launch for the *Chronicle*."

Tilda grabbed Isla's arm. "This. Is. Amazing!" she yelled. "Think of the publicity! We'll be able to fill up our booking sheet for a year."

"We'd better make a booking sheet then."

"I'm on it!" Tilda said, grabbing the laptop. "This is perfect, Isla. Poppy's Place is going to be *huge*!"

Chapter
Eight

Isla went into work with Mum on Saturday
morning to check on the abandoned cats.
She'd only visited a few times during the week
because she'd been so busy with homework,
and more secret meetings with Tilda, Milo
and Gran about Mum's birthday.

Isla approached the holding cages quietly.
The cats were still quite timid but they were
recovering well, and when they saw Isla, they
came to the cage door to greet her.

"How are you all today?" Isla asked, reaching her fingers through the bars.

The tortoiseshell cat licked her hand.

"Are you hungry?" Isla giggled.

Out of the four, he was the most inquisitive. The others – another boy with dark grey fur, and two ginger girls – were far more easily scared.

"Will they be ready to leave soon?" Isla asked Lucy when she came to feed the cats.

"I think so," Lucy said, holding up a large plastic syringe filled with a milky mixture. "Do you want to help me feed them?"

"Can I?" Isla asked.

Lucy nodded and handed Isla the syringe. Isla put it through the bars, holding it up to the tortoiseshell cat's mouth to let him lap at the mixture.

"We have to introduce soft food into their

diet slowly," Lucy told Isla.

"Where will they go when they're better? Could we have them at Poppy's Place?"

"They still have a lot of healing to do," Mum said, coming down the hallway carrying a guinea pig in her hands. "They need plenty of peace and quiet. I don't think a cat café would be the right place for that."

"Dolly doesn't have any space for them," Lucy said. "I checked."

Mum put the guinea pig in a nearby cage. "I guess if we took Oliver and a couple more cats, Dolly would have room for these four?"

Lucy looked at Mum, surprised. "It's a great idea. If you're sure?"

"You mean it?" Isla said, a little too loudly. "Sorry!" she whispered, as Mum pointed at the cats.

Mum nodded. "I know Dolly will take good

care of them. And to be honest, it seems like the only option. Right, Isla, we need to go home, I've got a couple of people coming to see the kittens."

"Already?" Isla asked.

"They're ready," Mum said. "It's time they went to their new homes."

That afternoon, Bonnie came over to meet Poppy and Roo and all the other cats. Mum had gone back to work after they'd said a slightly teary goodbye to Captain Snuggles and Fluffboy, and Isla had texted Grace to tell her she could pick up Lady Mewington.

Isla felt a bit shy at first – it had been Grace, Ayesha and her for so long – but Bonnie was so easy-going. It was good to have a new friend.

"You're so lucky," Bonnie said, stroking Benny.

"Do you have any pets?" Isla asked, hugging Lady Mewington, who seemed a bit lost without her brothers.

Milo had shut himself in his bedroom with Dynamo, worried that Mum might change her mind about keeping him, even though they'd all reassured him over and over again.

"No. It's just me and Dad in a small flat. There's not even enough room for a goldfish."

"You can visit Poppy's Place any time you like," Isla grinned. "No reservation needed."

"Thanks!" Bonnie said. "Oh, and I almost forgot…" She hunted through her bag and handed Isla a flat, neatly wrapped parcel covered in little black paw prints.

Inside was a new *I Heart Cats* notebook. "Oh!" Isla gasped. "You didn't have to."

"I noticed your other one was almost full."

"Thank you! Now I can make even more lists for Poppy's Place."

"I could help?" Bonnie offered.

"We need all the help we can get," Isla admitted. She gave Bonnie a sheepish grin. "Actually, how do you feel about cleaning?"

"I am sooo excited!" Grace cried as Isla opened the front door. "I've got everything ready."

She held up two huge bags full of cat toys and other accessories. "There's a cat bed, and kitten food, and a little fishing rod with a feather on the end, which is adorable! And look at this…" Grace held up a pink collar studded with tiny diamantes which spelled out *Lady M*. "Isn't it the cutest!"

Isla laughed. "You know you didn't need to bring all of that here…"

Grace looked at the bags and blushed. "I might have got a bit over-excited."

"Did you bring a carrier to take Lady Mewington home in?"

"I…" Grace smacked her hand against her forehead. "I knew I'd forgotten something!"

"Never mind," Isla said. "You can borrow one of ours. Are you staying for a while? Bonnie and I are cleaning out the conservatory."

Grace wrinkled her nose. "Um … OK … as

long as there's cake."

Isla laughed and headed for the kitchen. "Any chance of a tasty treat, Gran?"

Gran looked down at Poppy, who was half-asleep on her feet. "If Poppy will let me. I was just doing a bit of washing-up when she plopped herself down and fell asleep! I didn't have the heart to wake her."

Isla pulled over a chair so Gran could at least sit down while Poppy held her captive.

"Thanks, Isla. There's a Victoria sponge in the tin – I'll bring it through in a bit."

In the conservatory, they found Bonnie trying to sweep the floor, while Roo and Lady Mewington chased after the broom.

"Hi, Grace!" said Bonnie. "I've been playing with your gorgeous kitten. You're *so* lucky!"

Grace giggled in reply, then pulled a face as Isla handed her a duster.

Half an hour later, the room was looking spotless. Tilda came in clutching a mug of frothy coffee and sat down on a beanbag. "I've finally figured out the coffee machine!" she sighed. "Although who knows how it will work when we've got customers."

"You should have a trial run," Grace suggested, pretending to dust the table while she played with Lady Mewington.

"That's a great idea!" Isla said. "We can make sure everything runs smoothly so there'll be no disasters on the big day."

Tilda jumped up, almost spilling her coffee. "You're right!" she yelled. "Let's do it."

"I didn't mean now!" said Isla. "The crockery order hasn't arrived yet … neither have the tablecloths."

"Don't worry about that!" said Tilda, ushering Isla out of the room. "You go into town and get some stuff, and I'll stay here and get the conservatory ready."

"What about customers?" Bonnie asked.

Isla sighed. There was no point trying to change Tilda's mind. "I'll text Sam and tell him to come over with his friends," she said, grabbing her notebook. "They'd never turn down free cake."

"We need to shop smart," Isla told her friends as they took the bus into town.

Grace wrinkled her nose. "Shop smart?"

Isla shrugged. "It's something Tilda's always saying. We have to plan exactly what we need and where to get it from, so that we don't waste any time."

She giggled to herself – Tilda never shopped smart; she was always gone for hours.

Isla opened her new notebook and smiled at Bonnie. Together they made a list:

Poppy's Place Trial Run:
- *Cups and saucers (preferably cat-themed)*
- *Teapot and milk jug*
- *Napkins (see note above)*
- *Tablecloths*
- *Mats and coasters*

"Gran's given me some money, so we need to make sure we stay within budget."

The girls headed for one of the department stores and began their search. They found matching napkins and a tablecloth covered in kittens in the kitchen department, and Isla found some beautiful cat-themed mats and coasters, but there were no suitable tea sets. Everything was too expensive or *granny-ish* as Grace put it. In the end they gave up and headed for home, but as they were passing the parade of shops near Isla's house, Bonnie spotted something in the charity shop.

"Look!" she cried.

In the window was a tea set, painted with black and white cats who looked exactly like Poppy.

"It's perfect!" cried Isla. "And it was right on our doorstep all along!"

They arrived home to a hive of activity. Tilda had put herself in charge and looked more than happy as she ordered people about. Sam and his friends had come over early so Tilda had sent them into the garden to clean some chairs in the shed.

Gran and Milo were plating up a selection of cakes in the kitchen.

"We've agreed on a tasting menu," Tilda said, following Isla and her friends into the kitchen with her clipboard. "A little sample of what's to come when Poppy's Place opens for real."

"It all looks delicious," Grace said, licking her lips.

Isla, Grace and Bonnie set up the tables with the tablecloths, napkins and tea set they'd bought, and Tilda turned the coffee machine on and gave Gran a rushed tutorial on how to make a latte.

Finally, everything was ready – or as ready as it could be at such short notice. The customers – Sam, and his friends Tamar and Mark, and Grace and Bonnie – sat excitedly at the tables in the conservatory.

Isla and Tilda acted as waitresses, taking orders for tea and coffee and handing round taster plates full of sandwiches and delicious cakes.

"Wait!" Isla cried suddenly. "We've forgotten the most important thing."

Tilda stared at Isla blankly.

"The *cats*!" Isla said.

"I've got them," Mum said, herding Benny, Lady Mewington, Dynamo and Roo along the corridor. Poppy followed, coming to see what all the fuss was about.

Mum stopped in her tracks. She looked at the mess in the kitchen. "What's going on?" she asked Isla, suspiciously. "Why were the cats shut in the lounge?"

"We're having a trial run," Isla explained. "To see how the café would work and make sure there's nothing we've forgotten – we've got customers, too," she added as Mum peeked into the conservatory.

"What can I do?" Mum asked.

"Nothing," Isla said. "You're the guest of honour."

"Tilda," Gran called, "can you come and work the coffee machine?"

"Just press the blue button, Gran," Tilda shouted, steering Mum into the conservatory and plonking her down in a chair.

Isla followed with a pot of tea and a jug of

milk and started serving drinks. She was just
about to add milk to Sam's tea when there was
a shriek from the kitchen.

"Hey!" Sam cried, as Isla poured milk into
his lap.

"Sorry!" Isla blushed, handing him a cloth,
before hurrying out of the room after Tilda.

Gran stood in the
middle of the kitchen,
dripping with milk as
steam poured out of
the top of the coffee
machine. Benny,
Roo and Poppy
lapped at the pool
of milk at her feet.

"Are you OK?"
Isla asked.

"I think so,"

Gran said, wiping herself down with a towel. "Luckily the milk was still cold."

"You did press the blue button, didn't you?" Tilda asked.

"Yes, I'm sure I did … though I was a bit busy with the cakes, and Poppy wanted to help as well."

Poppy looked up at them with milk dripping from her whiskers and gave a meow.

"Well," said Gran. "Other than the milk incident, I think it's going quite well."

Isla nodded. "Everyone loves the tasting menu, and the cats seem quite happy with all the attention they're getting."

"I just hope nothing else goes wrong," Tilda said.

"It won't," Isla assured her. "Everything will go exactly according to plan – you'll see. Poppy's Place will be a huge success!"

The next week went by in a haze of activity. Mum called a family meeting on Monday night, and began by updating the whiteboard. She made two columns, one for the things which had already been done, and one for the things which still needed doing – one column was worryingly longer than the other...

"OK," she said, frowning at the list. "Let's start with the things we still need to buy." After much searching online, they found a fantastic website dedicated to cat-themed stuff, where they ordered tea towels, bunting, cushions, napkins and ten cat-shaped teapots.

Tilda showed them the updated website pages she'd been working on and gave an update on the RSVPs which included Julia and Bob from Cats, Cuddles and Cupcakes.

On Tuesday, Gran and Milo presented their final menu – complete with samples – and on Wednesday, Gran arranged for Mr Evans to come round when Isla got home from school so they could discuss the cat playground. Mr Evans was only too pleased to help and together they sketched out a design.

"I don't know when you're going to have time to build this," Mum said, peering over Isla's shoulder. "There's only two weeks to go."

"It's going to be hard to get it done for the launch," Mr Evans agreed. "But we'll do our best." He winked at Isla and she stifled a giggle – Mum had no idea of their secret plans!

Mum went back to her whiteboard. She seemed to have gone into overdrive – every spare minute was spent on the phone to suppliers and placing orders.

But by Friday, the two columns looked encouragingly even...

Chapter Nine

Isla woke early with butterflies in her tummy. It was Mum's birthday, and the first day of half-term. They had a big day ahead of them and Isla wanted to make sure that everything went perfectly. All their friends were coming over to help put *Operation Mum's Birthday* into action – including Ayesha's mum who was going to paint Mum her special mural.

Isla heard chatting in the kitchen and found Gran and Milo warming croissants and making tea for Mum in one of the new cat teapots.

"I'll wake Tilda," Isla said, "and make sure that Mum stays in bed."

As she'd expected, Isla found Mum already out of bed when she got to her room.

"The first rule of the day is that you relax!" Isla told her, leading Mum back to bed.

"Agreed," said Gran, as she, Milo and Tilda appeared in the doorway.

Mum laughed. "I'm not sure there should be rules on my birthday. Besides, I thought I'd make a start on the garden – it's a lovely day."

Isla and Tilda exchanged glances.

"Don't worry about that today," Gran said quickly, putting the breakfast tray down in front of Mum. "Forget all about Poppy's Place – this is a day for relaxing."

They all climbed on to Mum's bed. Isla

handed her a large, colourful bag, and watched excitedly as Mum opened her first present.

"Oh, they're … lovely," Mum said, a slightly confused look on her face as she held up a pair of flip-flops.

Tilda rolled her eyes at Isla. "I told you to give her the presents in order."

"Oops. Never mind," Isla told Mum. "It will make sense in a minute. Open the others."

"Mine next!" shouted Milo, passing Mum a messily wrapped package.

Mum opened it carefully to reveal a hand-made comic called *Super Cats Vs Deadly Dogz*, with four superhero kittens drawn on the front cover.

"That must be Dynamo," Mum said, pointing to a drawing of a kitten with a red mask, cape, and a bright blue "*D*" emblazoned across his chest.

"It's a first edition," Milo said proudly. "One day it will be worth loads of money."

Mum gave him a hug. "It's already priceless to me."

Next, Mum unwrapped a fluffy white dressing gown, and a new swimming costume.

"We've booked you on a spa day!" Isla explained.

"Nothing but rest and relaxation all day," Tilda ordered.

"With complimentary tea and cakes,"
Gran added, handing her a gift voucher.
"Everything's included."

"This is wonderful," said Mum. "But what
about the garden – it's like a jungle out there.
We can't open Poppy's Place with it looking
such a mess."

"Leave everything to us," Isla said sternly.

Mum gave Isla a teary smile. "I think this is
the best birthday I've ever had."

"Wait until you see the—" Milo started.

Isla put her hand over his mouth and
cut him off. "*Not yet,*" she whispered as he
struggled to get free.

While Mum headed off for her day of
pampering and relaxation, the rest of the

Palmers got started on the garden. As soon as Ayesha, Grace, Bonnie and Sam arrived, Isla put them straight to work on the weeds. She smiled to herself as she watched them chatting away. Tilda's advice to be herself had worked and she'd made a brilliant new friend.

Mr Evans brought over his lawnmower because they'd discovered that they didn't actually own one, and Gran and Milo filled pots with plants and flowers to go on the patio.

The chairs and tables had already had a bit of a clean up from their trial run, but some of them still looked rather shabby so Isla and Tilda gave them a fresh lick of paint.

"Roo! Stay away from the paint!" Isla cried as he tried to climb into a pot of bright green paint that Tilda had found in the shed. She didn't have time to deal with another paint disaster.

They stopped for a quick lunch, and in the afternoon Mr Evans and Sam started work on the cat playground, building wooden platforms for the cats to climb on.

"Is this fence OK for the mural?" Ayesha's mum asked, when she arrived.

"Yes please," Isla said, showing her a sketch she'd drawn. "I was thinking of something a bit like this?"

Ayesha's mum smiled. "That's lovely."

By late afternoon, they were all exhausted, but the garden was completely transformed.

"The cats are going to love it!" Isla said, looking at the little extra touches Mr Evans had added to the cat's play area.

"I think Roo already does!" Gran said as Roo bounded over and leaped on to a platform, followed closely by Poppy who sniffed at the bridge.

"It looks like a different garden," Isla said. "It's so much bigger. We could fit even more tables and chairs out here."

There was a call from inside the house as Mum arrived home from her spa day.

"She's here!" Isla could barely contain her excitement. She couldn't wait to see Mum's face when she saw everything they'd done.

Milo ran indoors, reappearing a few

moments later with a very relaxed-looking
Mum.

"Oh," said Mum, holding her hands to her
face as she saw the garden. "It's…"

"Amazing?" offered Isla.

"Fab?" said Tilda.

"Supersplenderiffic!" whooped Milo.

Mum nodded. "What Milo said. I can't
believe you did all this in a day!"

"And there's more," said Isla excitedly.
"Turn around."

Mum turned to look at the fence, which
was covered with a sheet. Tilda pulled it away
to reveal Ayesha's mum's mural. In the centre,
in bright blue paint, were the words *Poppy's
Place*, and perched on top of the letters were
all of the cats.

"There's space to add any new cats,"
Ayesha's mum said.

"And it'll be a lovely reminder of all the cats we help at Poppy's Place," said Isla.

Mum let out a small squeak. "It's beautiful."

She hugged Ayesha's mum so tightly, Isla thought she'd never let go.

Gran took Mum's hand. "There's one more thing."

She led Mum to the end of the garden, where she and Milo had planted a small silver birch tree. Beneath it was a little silver plaque which read: *In memory of Grandad*.

"He would have loved this," Mum said quietly.

The Palmers stood together, hand in hand, while everyone gathered around Grandad's tree. Isla missed him so much, but she also had so many wonderful memories of him.

She felt her heart swell with pride as she looked at all they'd achieved.

"Well," said Mum, wiping away a tear. "This is not a day I'm going to forget in a hurry. Thank you, all of you."

That evening, they went to their favourite Italian restaurant, where they stuffed themselves with pizza and talked about Grandad and how much he would have loved to have been a part of Poppy's Place. Isla couldn't remember seeing Mum or Gran – or any of them – so happy in a long time. Their plans for Poppy's Place were almost on schedule – just a few more finishing touches and they'd be ready for the big launch.

"I can't believe we're going to be open in a few days," Tilda said.

"I never thought that we could make it

happen." Mum smiled at each of them. "But you have – all of you – you've made it happen. Think of all the cats we'll be able to help – that's down to you. I'm so proud of you all."

"Are you going to cry again?" Milo asked, frowning.

Mum laughed. "I think I'm all cried out for today."

"I think we all are," said Gran.

After dinner, they walked home. Milo yawned as Mum opened the front door and Isla couldn't help yawn, too. It had been the most amazing day, but she felt absolutely exhausted.

"Ms Palmer!" a voice called from across the street.

Their neighbour Mrs Scott hurried over waving a large brown envelope. "I got some of your mail by accident," she said handing Mum the envelope. "I might have had it for a while, I'm afraid – I've been away on holiday for a week."

"It could be about the licence!" Isla said, feeling sick as Mum opened the envelope.

"It's a notice from the environmental health office," Mum said, looking at the date on the letter. "They must have sent this out last week. It says they're coming to inspect the café … tomorrow!"

Chapter Ten

Everyone was up early the next morning
to make sure there was no way they could
possibly fail the inspection. The letter said to
expect the inspector early in the afternoon,
but didn't give a specific time.

Isla helped Tilda set up the chairs and tables
in the conservatory and garden, even though
the weather didn't look all that promising. She
set the tables and put out the menus, and then
went to give Gran a hand in the kitchen. With

all the washing-up done and everything under control, she went in search of Mum. She found her scrubbing away at the windows in the conservatory in her dressing gown.

"We've already cleaned those," Isla told her. "Twice. Shouldn't you get dressed?" She glanced at Tilda, who had appeared in the doorway carrying some extra chairs.

Mum dunked the sponge so hard in the bucket that soapy water splashed all over her slippers. "He could be here at any moment."

"It's not the afternoon yet," Isla said.

Mum glanced at her watch. "It's nearly midday, Isla – that's the afternoon!"

"So much for her day of relaxation yesterday," Tilda muttered.

"I think we could all do with a little break," Gran said, carrying a tray of tea into the conservatory."

"And please don't worry," said Isla, sounding much more positive than she felt. "Hopefully this is just about ticking boxes."

For the first time since they'd started working on Poppy's Place, Isla was worried that they might not pull it off. They had to make sure the inspector couldn't find any reason to turn them down.

"I'm sure you're right," said Gran, handing Mum a cup of tea. "I've checked and double checked – the place is spotless."

Mum opened her mouth to protest, but Gran gave her the same stern look that Mum used on Milo, and she gave in.

Isla nodded. "Even the cats are glowing!"

She and Milo had brushed and groomed every cat until they practically sparkled.

"All we can do now is keep everything crossed," Isla said.

"What about the shed?" Mum said suddenly. "Has anyone checked in there?"

"He won't want to look in the shed!" Gran laughed.

Mum sighed. "I know you're all trying to help. I just don't know what we're going to do if we fail this inspection. Lucy is bringing Oliver and two more cats over today, after she drops off the rescue cats at Dolly's. This *has* to work, or we're going to end up with more cats than we started with!"

"Two more cats?" Tilda whispered to Isla. "Has she gone mad?"

Isla grinned. As far as she was concerned, they could never have too many cats.

"Is he here yet?" Milo asked, coming in from the garden.

"Take those muddy shoes off!" Mum yelled. "We haven't got time to clean the floor again."

Isla glanced at the clock on the wall. "Are we ready?"

Gran nodded. "As ready as we can be. The house is spotless. The garden looks better than I've ever seen it look, there's a chocolate sponge in the oven, and most important of all, we've finally mastered the coffee machine."

Isla looked at Mum. "You really should go and get dressed."

Mum gasped and ran upstairs to change.

Isla glanced round. "The café rules!" she said, running to fetch the sign they'd made.

Tilda had found an old piece of wood, and they'd decorated the edges, painting the rules in swirly lettering. There wasn't time to put it up, so Isla propped it up on a table in the centre of the room.

Just as Mum reappeared in her best dress, there was a loud knock at the door. Everyone froze. They stared at each other for a moment, none of them wanting to answer it.

"I'll go," Gran said finally.

The inspector was a serious-looking man with a thick black beard and thicker eyebrows, which hung over his eyes. He looked even more terrifying than Isla had imagined.

"I'm Ms Palmer," Mum said, shaking the inspector's hand.

"Mr Black," he said. "Shall we start in the tea room first?"

He opened his briefcase, and brought out a clipboard and red pen.

"We have tables and chairs in the conservatory, and in the garden for when the weather is a bit nicer," Mum said, clearing her throat.

They all looked out to the garden. Unfortunately it had started to pour with rain. The inspector followed their gaze and frowned, jotting down some notes. Isla was sure she'd seen him mark something with a cross, so she gave him her best smile.

"Does it look OK so far?" she asked, her voice coming out in a squeak as she leaned closer to get a peek at his paperwork.

He pulled the clipboard to his chest. "I'm afraid I can't tell you anything until I have finished the inspection."

Isla shrugged at Mum as they all trooped after Mr Black into the kitchen.

"When are you planning to open?" he asked.

"Saturday," Mum replied. "We hope," she added in a whisper.

Isla could see that Mum had her fingers crossed behind her back, so she did the same.

"The food will be prepared in here?" he asked, watching as a soaking wet Roo skidded across the floor with Dynamo chasing after him.

Isla scooped them up and handed Dynamo to Milo. "Sorry!" she said grabbing a cloth to wipe away the muddy paw prints. "He's been playing in the rain."

"I think you'll find everything is up to

standard," Gran said.

The inspector nodded. "What…" he looked down at Poppy, distracted. She was purring loudly, and winding herself around his legs.

Isla suddenly had a terrible thought – *what if Mr Black hated cats?* She clicked her fingers to get Poppy's attention so that she'd leave Mr Black alone.

"What will you be doing with the cats while the café is open?" asked Mr Black.

"What do you mean?" Gran asked, looking confused.

"Obviously, they can't be anywhere near the food preparation area. What do you plan to do with them?"

"They'll be in the conservatory with the customers," Mum stuttered. "That's the whole point of a cat café."

Mr Black raised his eyebrows in surprise. "A cat café? I have nothing in my paperwork about a cat café."

He pulled a sheet from his clipboard and showed it to Mum – it was a printout of the form Tilda and Gran had filled in online. He pointed at a line which clearly said: *Application to open a café.*

"There must be some mistake," Gran told him.

"Our online system very rarely makes mistakes," said Mr Black.

"Tilda?" Mum said. "Do you remember what you put on the application?"

Tilda's cheeks went pink. "There wasn't an option for a cat café," she said. "So I clicked on the closest thing."

Mr Black put his pen and clipboard back into his briefcase and sighed. "I'm afraid, if the application has not been correctly filled out, there's nothing more I can do here."

"But … did we pass the inspection?" Mum asked.

"You probably would have," Mr Black admitted. "But the addition of cats changes things. There are different regulations for businesses concerning animals. You're going to have to fill out a new set of forms."

"How long will that take?" Isla asked, squeezing Milo's hand tightly as his lip wobbled, and feeling like she might burst into tears at any moment, too.

"It can take up to two weeks to process an application," Mr Black said. "Even then, I'm not sure you'll be approved. Cat cafés are rather out of the ordinary, so there'll need to be another inspection—" He paused, seeing the devastated look on Isla's face, and his own face softened. "I'm sorry, but without all of the necessary paperwork and a satisfactory inspection Poppy's Place won't be able to open on Saturday."

Chapter
Eleven

It turned out that Mr Black did like cats, so
Isla couldn't feel too upset with him, even
though she had to fight back tears at the
thought of Poppy's Place not being allowed
to open. She took him through to the
conservatory to meet the other cats, while
Gran cut him a slice of chocolate cake and
Tilda made a cup of coffee.

He seemed particularly fond of Benny. "She
reminds me of the cat we had when I was a

child," said Mr Black. "Her name was Buzz."

Milo laughed at the name until Isla told Mr Black the names Milo had given the kittens. Mr Black grinned and kneeled down to stroke Poppy, who held her paw up to him.

"What a clever cat!"

"She can do lots more tricks," Milo said.

"Tell me more about your cat café," he said. "I've never been to one before."

Isla told him all about the cat cafés in Japan and how they'd had the idea to open their own home-made cat café to help find homeless cats a forever home. Mr Black sat on the sofa to eat his cake and Benny soon settled herself on to his lap, purring loudly.

"It's such a great idea," he said, stroking Benny. "I love cats, but I live on the fifteenth floor of a block of flats. Not the best place to keep a cat."

"Isn't there anything we can do so that we can still open on time?" Gran asked.

Isla gave Mr Black a pleading look as she cuddled up with Roo on the beanbag.

The inspector thought for a moment. "Let me show you which form you need to fill out. If you print it out and fill it in now, I'll take it back to the office with me. I can't make any promises, but I'll do my best to make sure your application goes to the top of the pile."

"Really?" said Mum. "That would be brilliant, thank you so much."

Mr Black smiled. "No, thank you. I'd

forgotten how relaxing it is to have a cat."

Mum beamed at Isla who gave her a thumbs up. "Better get started then."

Before he left, Mr Black gave them a checklist of everything they had to do to make sure that the café passed the next inspection, now that they were being re-inspected as a cat café.

"The earliest I could come back to do the inspection is Friday afternoon," he told them. "But that depends on the application being processed in time. Let's all keep our fingers crossed," he said, giving Benny a final stroke before heading for his car.

"Do you think we can do it?" Isla asked Mum the next day.

She'd tossed and turned all night thinking about the inspection.

"I don't know," Mum admitted, showing her the checklist. "There's a lot on here that I didn't even consider – customer access, health and safety stuff to do with the cats…"

"At least Mr Black is on our side," Isla said.

"It's not up to Mr Black," Mum told her. "Even with his help, the form might not get processed in time." She took Isla's hand. "I know it's not what you want to hear, but I think we may have to cancel the grand opening."

"We can't!" Tilda said, coming into the lounge with a big box full of flyers. "Look how far we've come. We can't give up at the last minute."

"We're not giving up, Tilda," Mum said. "But we can't open without a licence."

"We'll get it. I know we will." Tilda

gestured to the box. "I'm going to hand out flyers with Gabriella and Eloise. We still have to promote Poppy's Place."

As she opened the front door, she met Lucy on the doorstep holding two cat carriers. "Cat delivery!" Lucy sang. "Meet the newest moggy members of Poppy's Place."

Mum groaned and put her head in her hands.

Lucy placed the carriers carefully on the floor and looked at their glum faces. "What's the matter? How did the inspection go?"

"Not so great," Gran said, explaining what had happened.

Isla and Milo peeked in at the new arrivals.

"I recognize Oliver," Isla said, opening one of the cat carriers to lift a sleepy Oliver out for a hug. She peeped inside the other carrier. "But who are these two?"

The cats were maybe two years old at the most, with silky black fur and bright green eyes.

"The one with the little white spot above his nose is Albert, and the other one is Victoria," Lucy said.

"Of course! We met them on our visit. They're gorgeous!" Isla said, wiggling her fingers through the door of the carrier.

"Don't get too attached," Mum warned. "We're definitely not keeping any more cats. This is temporary – until they find their forever homes."

Isla grinned. She wouldn't get attached – at least, she'd *try* not to – but she was still planning to give them lots of love and attention while they were there.

Roo wandered over to the cat carrier and gave a little meow, batting at Albert's tail, which poked out of the carrier door.

"Let's take them into the conservatory," Isla told Milo, handing him Oliver, and lifting the carrier containing Albert and Victoria. "Come and meet your new house guests," Isla told Poppy as she followed after them.

Poppy was like a mother to all the cats. She'd been there to welcome every single one as they'd arrived at the Palmers.

Milo put Oliver down and he wandered beneath a chair where he curled up and promptly fell fast asleep.

"I knew he would love it here," Isla said. "It's the perfect home for him."

"I don't even really like cats," Milo joked.

Isla giggled. "Me neither."

Wednesday and Thursday flew by in a whirlwind of cleaning, ironing tablecloths, and making table decorations, as they tried to make everything perfect in the hope of Mr Black's return visit. By the time Friday arrived, Isla felt so excited and nervous she could hardly sit still.

To keep herself busy, Isla decided to start on the cat profiles for Oliver, Albert and Victoria. She had been surprised at how quickly they'd settled in. Oliver had found a favourite spot beneath the radiator in the kitchen and occasionally peeped one eye open to see what was going on, but otherwise he slept most of the time.

Victoria and Albert both seemed eager to get out into the garden. Isla thought it was probably because they were used to having an entire farm to roam around in, but Mum said they had to stay inside until they got used to their new surroundings.

Isla found them curled up next to each other in the conservatory and sat down to stroke them. They were both so beautiful – Isla was sure they would be adopted quickly.

She wandered into the kitchen and sat down at the table between Tilda and Mum.

"Well, if we don't get the go-ahead we can at least have a party with our friends and the cats," Tilda said as she worked away at her laptop. "We've got fifty RSVPs for the grand opening. That's not including Sally Smithers and whoever she brings with her."

"Fifty!" Mum said. "How on earth are we going to fit fifty people in the conservatory?"

"There's the garden as well," Tilda said.

"Let's just hope it doesn't rain then," Gran muttered.

Tilda printed out a copy of the guest list along with the final menus. She popped them into the cat-shaped stands on the tables, then glanced at the clock.

"I've just got to nip into town to pick something up," she said mysteriously. She grabbed her hoodie and disappeared out of the door before anyone could ask any questions.

"Do you know what that was about?" Mum asked.

"No idea," said Isla, wondering what her sister was up to. Hopefully she'd let her in on the secret later.

Isla had invited Grace, Ayesha and Bonnie over in the afternoon to help out with the finishing touches. As soon as they arrived they started work on the front window. Gran had made some beautiful new curtains covered in a colourful cat pattern, and Ayesha had brought a Poppy's Place sign that her mum had painted to go in the window.

"What about the side gate?" Ayesha asked.

Isla gasped. "We didn't make a bigger sign!"

"There's still time," Grace said.

"Let's make one now," said Bonnie.

They spent the afternoon painting a sign for the gate, using the mural for inspiration. Isla added the new cats to the scene as well, then they hung it carefully with a hammer and nails.

"Perfect!" Isla said looking at her watch. "Let's keep our fingers crossed that Mr Black can make it."

"Do you think he'll come?" Isla asked Mum an hour later, pacing the kitchen floor anxiously with Roo chasing back and forth after her to get her attention. Grace, Ayesha and Bonnie had gone home, and Isla had spent every minute since walking between the front window looking for Mr Black and the kitchen to see if Mum or Gran had any news.

"He did say he couldn't make any promises, Isla," Gran said gently.

"When's dinner?" Milo wailed, clutching his stomach as he rolled on the floor. "I'm starving!"

"I'll make a start on the chicken pie," Gran said. "It is getting rather late."

The front door slammed open suddenly, making Roo – and Isla – jump.

"Has he been? Did we pass?" Tilda yelled.

Mum shook her head.

"We failed?" Tilda whispered, her face white.

"He didn't come," Isla said. "And we're out of time."

They barely touched the chicken pie Gran made for dinner, apart from Milo who was only too happy to have an extra helping. Mum was about to suggest they all had an early night when the phone rang. They sat in silence, listening to Mum's muffled voice in the next room.

"That was Mr Black," Mum said, when she got off the phone. "He was on his way here when his car broke down. He said he'll try his best to do the inspection first thing in the morning, but can't make any promises. He did say that he'd fast-tracked the forms though, and they've all been processed."

"Doesn't he have a mobile?" Tilda asked.

"He does, but the battery died after the tow truck picked him up," Mum said.

"So now it's all down to the inspection?" Isla asked.

Mum nodded. "We pass that and we'll get our licence."

Chapter
Twelve

"Right," said Mum. "We open at three o'clock. Does everyone know what they're doing?"

It was only nine o'clock, but they'd been up for hours, unable to sleep.

"I'm baking with Gran," said Milo, rolling out some dough on the kitchen counter.

"I'm at the entrance welcoming guests," said Tilda, holding up her clipboard.

"I'm on cat duty and waitressing when the guests arrive," said Isla.

She'd also enlisted the help of Grace, Bonnie and Ayesha. When Poppy's Place opened for real they would only be accepting a maximum of ten customers at one time. But as Tilda had invited practically everyone they knew to the launch, it was going to be a lot more work. There was no way Isla would be able to do it all by herself.

"What will you be doing?" Milo asked Mum.

"I'm going to be hiding upstairs until it's all over," she joked.

"You're the host," Isla told her. "Introducing everyone to the cats at Poppy's Place and telling them about all the good work we're going to do."

Mum took a deep breath. "OK. We can do this. Mr Black said he'd try to get here by ten o'clock."

"Come on, Milo, we'd better get the oven on," Gran said.

"Wait!" cried Isla, hearing a knock. "There's someone at the door."

Mr Black had kept his word. "I hope I'm not too early," he said. "Are you ready?" They all nodded. "Then I'll begin."

Mr Black walked slowly from room to room, inspecting everything from the downstairs toilet just off the hallway, to every single cupboard and drawer in the kitchen, making notes as he went. Isla couldn't bear the suspense, so she went into the garden to check on Poppy and Roo, who were playing on the new cat playground.

It was a beautiful autumn day so they'd put out chairs and tables on the patio. Lucy was going to keep an extra close eye on the cats to make sure that none of them got scared during the party, but as they were free to go where they wanted, Isla was sure that wouldn't be a problem.

"Oh," said Mr Black, coming outside. "It's lovely out here. That looks like a lot of fun," he said, looking at the cats leaping across the platforms and playing with the toys.

He wrote something on his clipboard,

 giving Isla a little smile, and returned inside.

Isla stroked Poppy as she came to stand beside her on the grass.

"I hope this works, Poppy," Isla whispered. "Victoria and Albert deserve to find their forever home."

Poppy rubbed her head against Isla's knee

and gave a little meow.

Isla smiled. "You really are a special cat."

After a while, Isla crept back into the house. Mr Black was with Mum and Gran, scribbling down a last few notes in the kitchen.

"Well?" she asked, trying to keep her voice steady.

Mr Black ripped a sheet of paper from his clipboard and handed it to Mum with a frown.

"I can't look," Mum said.

Mr Black handed it to Isla. She took the sheet, her hands shaking. It had a single word scrawled across it in big red letters.

"It says … congratulations!"

Isla looked at Mr Black whose face lit up with a huge smile.

"You passed!" he told them. "Poppy's Place can open."

Mum took the piece of paper from Isla and

stared at it, shaking her head as though she could hardly believe her eyes. "We can open?" she asked. "No more forms to fill out?"

Mr Black laughed. "No more forms. You might have an inspection every few months initially, but otherwise you're all set."

"We passed!" Milo whooped, bouncing around the house. "We passed, we passed!"

"We passed?" Tilda shrieked, running down the stairs. "I knew it! What did I tell you?"

Isla stood there, speechless. It was really going to happen!

"Thank you," said Mum, shaking Mr Black's hand. "For everything."

Mr Black blushed. "I was hoping I might be able to come back for the opening? It all sounds very exciting, and I'd love to spend more time with the cats. I've been considering moving to a new house," he said. "Maybe adopting a cat of my own – your cats have brought back so many memories."

"Well," said Mum with a smile. "If it's cats you're after, you've come to the right place."

"I've got you a present," Tilda told Isla, as they prepared to open the doors to their very first customers.

"Is this what you went to pick up yesterday?" Isla asked, clutching her hands together to stop them shaking. She'd never felt so excited or nervous. Her dream had finally come true – Poppy's Place was about to open. She glanced out at the garden – it looked perfect, even the sun was shining.

Grace, Bonnie and Ayesha were in their places in the conservatory, ready to take orders. Milo and Gran were putting the finishing touches to the cakes, and Mum was doing a last-minute check on the cats so that she knew where each of them was.

Oliver and Dynamo were being kept upstairs away from all the people and the noise. Mum had let Albert and Victoria into the garden, as they seemed desperate to get outside to play with Roo and Benny, and Poppy had been sticking close to Isla all day, as though sensing her nervousness.

Tilda nodded and handed her a bag. Isla peered inside and found two bright blue T-shirts.

"There's one for me, and one for you," Tilda said excitedly.

Isla pulled out one of the T-shirts to find the Poppy's Place logo printed on the front adorned with her cat doodles.

"I love it! It's amazing!" Isla said, giving Tilda a hug. "Don't let anyone in yet. I want to put this on first."

She ran to her bedroom and quickly changed, admiring herself in the mirror before hurrying downstairs.

"Ready?" Tilda asked, wearing her T-shirt, too, as they walked back out to the garden.

"Ready," said Isla.

"Ready," said Mum, giving them both a hug.

They took up their positions and Tilda opened the gate to a sea of faces. At the front of the line was Sam and some of his friends.

"We couldn't miss this," he told Isla, as he showed his friends the cat playground he'd helped to make.

Isla recognized so many familiar faces – friends and neighbours, Lucy and clients of Abbey Park Vets. And everyone looked so excited to be there.

By the time Sally Smithers arrived, the party was in full swing and the cats were loving all the attention – Isla was sure that she saw Roo gobbling up little bits of cake from the floor. Ayesha, Grace and Bonnie were rushed off their feet taking orders and serving tea and coffee and cake. And best of all was the laughter – wherever she went, Isla could hear the happy sound of laughter.

"Your table is this way, Miss Smithers," Isla said, showing the journalist to one of the tables in the garden. She handed her a menu. "I can recommend the chocolate cake!"

"My favourite!" Sally grinned. "That and a cup of tea please."

Tilda streaked by, dashing towards the house. "I'll be back in a minute. I've forgotten the *most* important thing."

She returned seconds later clutching a pair of scissors and a huge red ribbon which she strung across the garden from one fence to the other.

"What's that?" Isla asked.

"It's for the grand opening," Tilda told Isla. "Go and find Mum."

Isla brought Mum into the garden, as Tilda clambered on to a chair.

"Can I have everyone's attention, please!"

she shouted, handing Mum the scissors. "It's time for the grand opening."

"As much as I would love the honour," Mum said, looking at Isla, "I think that Poppy's Place should be officially opened by the person who started all of this, and who never stopped believing that we would have our very own home-made cat café – even when things went a bit wrong."

Isla blushed, as everyone laughed.

"She knew that we could make a difference, not just to the lives of these wonderful cats, but to humans as well."

Mum gestured to Benny who was snuggled up on Mr Black's lap, then to Milo trying to hold on to a wriggly Roo, and to Poppy, who was weaving herself around Isla's legs.

"Isla," Mum said, handing her the scissors. "Would you do us the honour?"

Isla held the scissors in her shaky hands, grinning from ear to ear. Then she took a deep breath and announced, "I hereby declare Poppy's Place … open!"

As she cut the ribbon there was a huge cheer and a round of applause. Mum gave Isla a hug, then Tilda, Milo and Gran joined them and Poppy wound around their feet.

"We did it!" Mum said, wiping away a tear.

"It's better than I ever imagined," Isla said.

"I'm not sure I'd want this many people
here every day," said Gran, laughing. "We're
run off our feet!"

"Better get used to being busy," Tilda said,
showing them her clipboard. "We've already
got four bookings for tomorrow."

"Tomorrow!" Mum squealed.

Isla grinned. "Tomorrow we start for real."

Isla couldn't believe that they'd done it. After all the dramas and emergencies … not to mention exhausting hard work, they had pulled it off. She looked around at the smiling faces, and thought of Albert and Victoria, and all the cats they'd help in the future to find their forever homes.

"It all starts now," Isla said, scooping up Poppy into a hug. Poppy's Place was open for business.

KATRINA CHARMAN

Katrina lives in the middle of South East England with
her husband and three daughters. She has wanted to
be a children's writer ever since she was eleven, when
she was set the task of writing an epilogue to Roald
Dahl's *Matilda*. Her teacher thought her writing was
good enough to send to Roald Dahl himself. Sadly
Katrina never got a reply, but the experience ignited
her love of reading and writing.

Tweet Katrina: @katrina_charman

LUCY TRUMAN

Since graduating from Loughborough University
with a degree in Illustration, Lucy has become one
of the UK's leading commercial illustrators. Lucy
draws inspiration from popular culture, fashion and
all things vintage to create her fabulous artworks.
This, combined with her love of people-watching,
allows Lucy to create illustrations which encapsulate
aspirational everyday living.

Tweet Lucy: @iLucyT

Find out how Poppy's Place began in...

Poppy's Place

THE HOME-MADE
CAT CAFÉ

ILLUSTRATED BY
LUCY TRUMAN

KATRINA CHARMAN

Isla Palmer is CRAZY about cats - SUPER-IN-LOVE crazy - but her vet nurse mum has never let her have one. Then Isla meets Poppy, a gorgeous cat in need of a loving home, and comes up with the perfect way to convince Mum. It's not long before Poppy has transformed life at the Palmers' - everyone is happier, especially Gran, and even Isla's older sister Tilda admits she likes having Poppy around. But Poppy isn't the only one in need of a home and soon their house is full of cats. With Mum at her wits' end, Isla needs to come up with a plan - and fast!

Poppy's Place

Trouble AT THE CAT CAFÉ

Cat café or total CAT-ASTROPHE?

Join in the fun at
#POPPYSPLACE
Tweet @stripesbooks